TOU-CAN'T!

A Little Sister Story

BY **BRANDON TODD**

PHILOMEL BOOKS

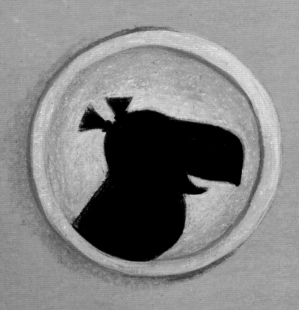

PHILOMEL BOOKS
An imprint of Penguin Random House LLC, New York

First published in the United States of America by Philomel,
an imprint of Penguin Random House LLC, 2021.

Philomel Books is a registered trademark of Penguin Random House LLC.

Visit us online at penguinrandomhouse.com.

Library of Congress Cataloging-in-Publication Data is available.

Manufactured in China

ISBN 9780593117637

10 9 8 7 6 5 4 3 2 1

Edited by Talia Benamy.
Design by Ellice M. Lee.
Text set in Neutraface.
The art was created with colored pencils and Adobe Photoshop.

For Wren and all the big (and little) things you will do

I am little.

My sister reminds me
of that fact every day.

She ties her own shoes.

She makes her own breakfast.

She reads books by herself.

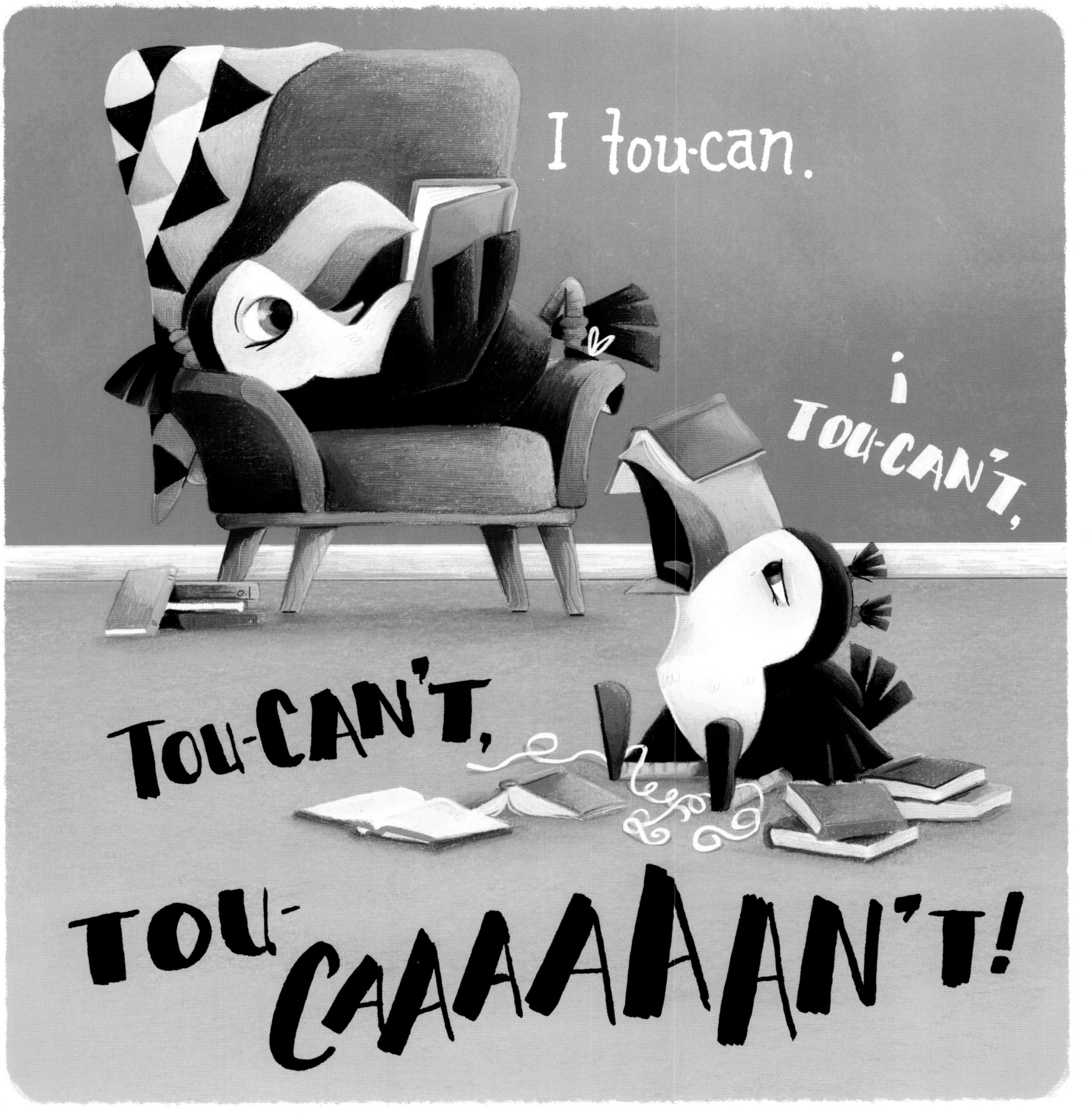
I tou-can.
i TOU-CAN'T,
TOU-CAN'T,
TOU-CAAAAAN'T!

i WANT
TO BE
BiG.

I've tried stretching.

I've tried wearing her shoes.

I've even tried eating her food.

CAN'T!

IT'S NOT FAIR THAT I'M LITTLE.

I want to stay up late and watch scary movies . . .

and reach the candy bowl on top of the fridge . . .

and go to school all day. Just like her.

My sister looks smaller today.

I help get her slippers.

I help get her snacks.

I tell her a good night story.

I tou-can't.

¡TOU-CAN!

Being big is hard work.

I think I deserve a reward.

I think I'm done being big now.

I am little.

My sister *still* reminds me.

But I know it's the little things

that matter the most.

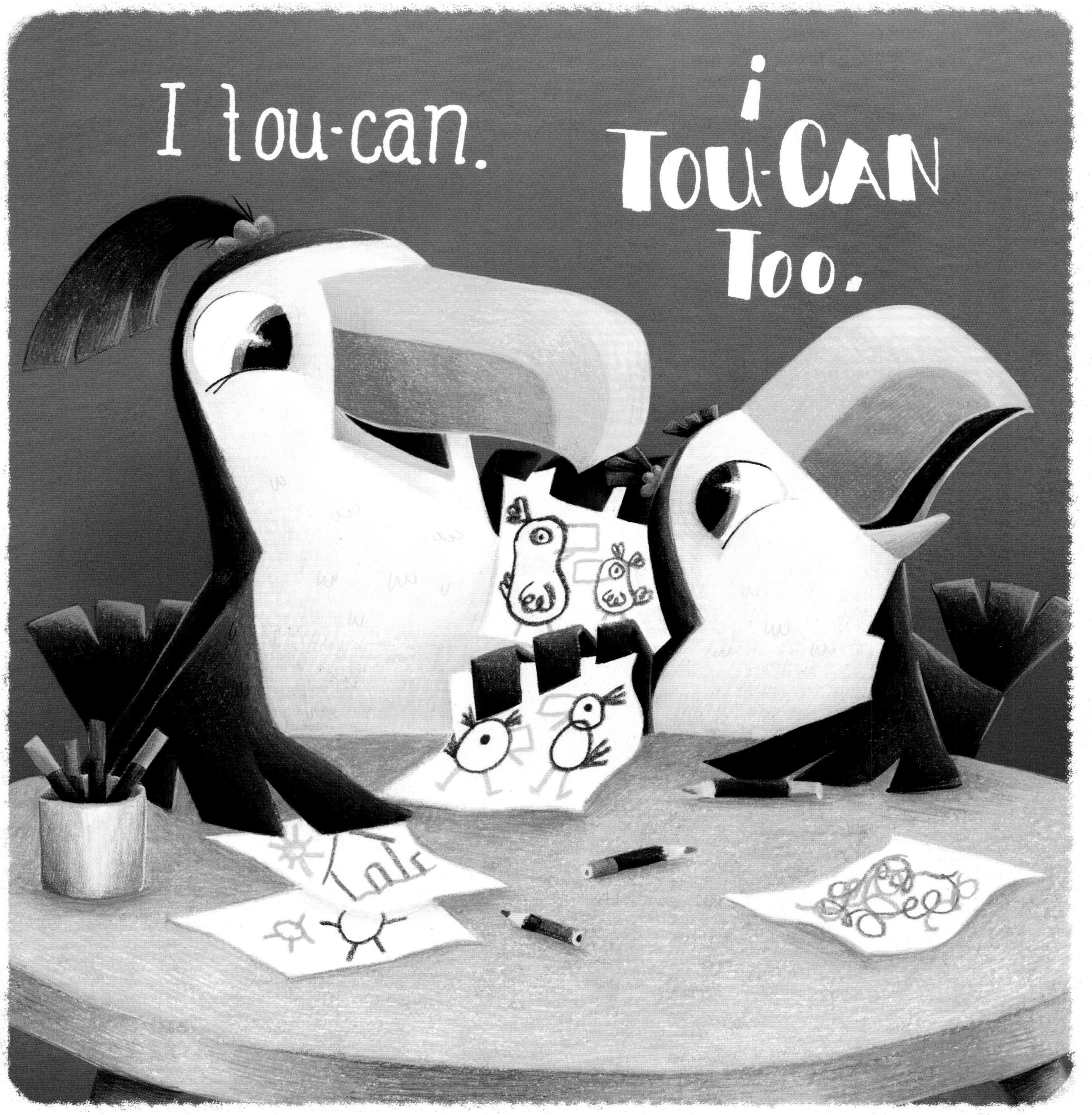
I tou-can.
I TOU-CAN TOO.